Alienne
The Musical Adventures of My Little Martian

Book, Music & Lyrics
by Jim Colleran

ISBN 978-0-573-71173-2

www.concordtheatricals.com
www.concordtheatricals.co.uk

No one shall make any changes in this title(s) for the purpose of production. No part of this book may be reproduced, stored in a retrieval system, scanned, uploaded, or transmitted in any form, by any means, now known or yet to be invented, including mechanical, electronic, digital, photocopying, recording, videotaping, or otherwise, without the prior written permission of the publisher. No one shall share this title(s), or any part of this title(s), through any social media or file hosting websites.

For all inquiries regarding motion picture, television, online/digital and other media rights, please contact Concord Theatricals Corp.

MUSIC AND THIRD-PARTY MATERIALS USE NOTE

Licensees are solely responsible for obtaining formal written permission from copyright owners to use copyrighted music and/or other copyrighted third-party materials (e.g. artworks, logos) in the performance of this play and are strongly cautioned to do so. If no such permission is obtained by the licensee, then the licensee must use only original music and materials that the licensee owns and controls. Licensees are solely responsible and liable for clearances of all third-party copyrighted materials, including without limitation music, and shall indemnify the copyright owners of the play(s) and their licensing agent, Concord Theatricals Corp., against any costs, expenses, losses and liabilities arising from the use of such copyrighted third-party materials by licensees. For music, please contact the appropriate music licensing authority in your territory for the rights to any incidental music.

IMPORTANT BILLING AND CREDIT REQUIREMENTS

If you have obtained performance rights to this title, please refer to your licensing agreement for important billing and credit requirements.

ALIENNE: THE MUSICAL ADVENTURES OF MY LITTLE MARTIAN premiered at The New York International Fringe Festival on August 9, 2014. The performance was co-directed by Jim Colleran and Joanna Greer and choreographed by Joanna Greer, with sets and lighting by Steve O'Shea, costumes by Megan Turek, and props by Justin Perkins. The Production Stage Manager was Chelsea Parrish. The cast was as follows:

KING NEBULA . . . . Robert Charles Russell

ALIENNE . . . . Jenna Dallacco

COSMINA . . . . Maria Pedro

TIM . . . . Joe Chisholm

SPROCKET . . . . Daniel Moser

EARTHSULA . . . . Tauren Hagans

QUARK . . . . .Gerardo Pelati

CHARACTERS

QUEEN/KING NEBULA – Any gender. Ruler of Mars. Imperious, haughty, noble, unyielding.

ALIENNE – Female. Nebula's teenage daughter. Spunky, optimistic, resourceful, brave.

COSMINA – Female. Alienne's best friend. Trendy, hip, astute, no-nonsense.

TIM – Male. Human amateur astronomer. Intelligent, affable, wistful, sincere.

SPROCKET – Any gender. Tim's robot companion. Sarcastic, dry, sesquipedalian.

EARTHSULA – Female. Evil space witch. Wicked, impatient, powerful, fabulous. Quark says she looks like a professional wrestler.

QUARK – Any gender. Earthsula's hench creature. Goofy, content, appealingly dumb. Quark could be anything: A furry pet? A rock-like gnome? A lizard? Doesn't matter, as long as Quark is funny.

MARSHA – Martian narrator

MARLA – Martian narrator

MARGO – Martian narrator

MARTY – Martian narrator

MARLIN – Martian narrator

ENSEMBLE – Martians, Partygoers, Ancestors, and Narrators

In a cast of seven actors, **COSMINA**, **SPROCKET**, **TIM**, and **QUARK** double as **MARTIAN NARRATORS**, and **NEBULA**, **SPROCKET**, **TIM**, and **QUARK** double as **ANCESTORS**.

The role of **NEBULA** is written as a queen singing in an alto range. If a male performer is cast in the role, licensees may feel free to change the pronouns and references to "king," "father," "sir," etc. Tracks and guide vocal recordings in baritenor keys are also available upon request.

SETTING

Mars and Earth.

TIME

The not-too-distant past.

MUSICAL NUMBERS

Scene One: The Prologue
1.   Opening. . . . . Instrumental
2.   My Little Martian . . . . .Martians
2a. My Little Martian (Reprise 1) . . . . Martians & Ensemble

Scene Two: The Party
3.   The Martian Ball . . . . Nebula, Martians & Partygoers
3a. My Little Martian (Reprise 2). . . . . . . Martians & Ensemble

Scene Three: Alienne's Wish
4.   The Earthling Stomp . . . . Cosmina & Ancestors
4a. My Little Martian (Reprise 3). . . . . Cosmina & Ancestors
5.   I Wanna Be a Human. . . . . Alienne

Scene Four: Tim's Wish
6.   I Wanna Meet a Martian & Duet . . . . Tim & Alienne

Scene Five: The Deal
7.   Spell #1 . . . . Earthsula
7a. My Little Martian (Reprise 4). . . . . . . Martians & Ensemble
7b. I Wanna Be a Human (A Cappella) . . . . Alienne
8.   Space Witch . . . . Earthsula, Quark & Ensemble
9.   Spell #2 . . . . Earthsula
10. Space Witch (Reprise) . . . . . . Earthsula, Quark & Ensemble
10a. My Little Martian (Reprise 5). . . . . . . Martians & Ensemble

Scene Six: The Meeting
11. Catch the Moon . . . . Alienne, Tim, Martians & Ensemble

Scene Seven: The Reaction
12. Alienne. . . . . Nebula & Cosmina
13. Spell #3 . . . . Earthsula & Quark
13a. My Little Martian (Reprise 6). . . . . . . Martians & Ensemble
13b. My Little Martian (Reprise 7). . . . . . . Martians & Ensemble
14. The Solar Eclipse, Part 1. . . . . Martians & Ensemble
14a. The Solar Eclipse, Part 2 . . . . Martians & Ensemble

Scene Eight: The Confrontation

Scene One: The Prologue

[MUSIC NO. 01 – OPENING]

(**MARTY** *enters humming, sees audience and reacts with surprise.)*

MARTY. Whoa! Hey, Marsha! Marsha the Martian!! Get out here!

MARSHA. *(Entering.)* Okay, okay...what is it, Marty?

MARTY. Check it out: Earthlings!

MARSHA. I can't believe it! We better tell everyone, Marty. *(Calls offstage.)* Marnie! Margo! Marlin! You've gotta see this.

MARNIE, MARGO & MARLIN. *(Ad-lib.)* What? What's all the fuss?

MARSHA. Get a look at this... we've got an Earthling audience out here, and they're expecting a Martian extravaganza!

MARNIE. Whoa... an *all*-Earthling audience? I can't believe it. We haven't had one of those in a comet's age!

MARTY. Well, we've got one now, so brush up on your Earth-speak. *(Aside.)* And speak slowly... you know how simple those Earthlings can be.

MARSHA. Now, now...be nice. No one in the universe thinks that way anymore.

MARGO. Maybe not. But there certainly was a time when Earthlings were considered the lowest of the low.

MARLIN. The gutter of the Galaxy.

MARNIE. The yuck of the Universe.

MARSHA. Enough. All that has changed, thank the stars.

MARGO. I do remember one particular story, however...

MARLIN. Back when humans were the "out" in "outer space."

MARTY. Yes, there was one particular Martian who wanted something more...

MARSHA. Ah, I remember her, too. Little Alienne...

MARTIANS. My little Martian!!

[MUSIC NO. 02 – MY LITTLE MARTIAN]

MY LITTLE MARTIAN,
LONG AGO AND FAR AWAY...
MY LITTLE MARTIAN,
THAT'S THE TALE WE'RE TELLING TODAY!

MARTY. Hey, I have an idea. Audience, you can help us tell our story. Any time someone says, "my little Martian," you help us sing that theme song.

MARSHA. Great idea! Let's practice once to get it right.

> (**MARTIANS** *teach the audience the song and movements.*)

MARNIE. And now, it is our pleasure to present...

MARTIANS. *Alienne: The Musical Adventures of...My Little Martian!*

[MUSIC NO. 02A – MY LITTLE MARTIAN (REPRISE 1)]

> (**ENSEMBLE MARTIANS** *enter, joining.*)

MY LITTLE MARTIAN,
LONG AGO AND FAR AWAY...
MY LITTLE MARTIAN,
THAT'S THE TALE WE'RE TELLING TODAY!

Scene Two: The Party

MARGO. It all began at one of Queen Nebula's Universe-famous parties.

MARLIN. Life forms came from all over just to hang out with the Queen.

MARSHA. And believe us, those

[MUSIC NO. 03 – THE MARTIAN BALL]

space creatures know how to party!

NEBULA.
DON'T WASTE YOUR TIME AT THE GALAXY MALL,
COME ONE, COME ALL, TO THE MARTIAN BALL.
WE'VE GOT PULSAR PUNCH AND SOLAR SNACKS
AT THE MARTIAN BALL!

MARTY.
WITH THE ALL-STAR, SPACED-OUT, BIG-BANG BAND

MARSHA.
AND THE LITTLE DIPPER DANCERS TO LEND A HAND,

MARNIE, MARGO & MARLIN.
WE'LL GIVE THAT DANCE FLOOR QUITE A WAX,

MARTIANS.
AT THE MARTIAN BALL!

NEBULA.
SO, GATHER YOUR SQUAD AND BEAM YOURSELF OVER!
USE A ROCKET, A POD, OR A LUNAR ROVER!

NEBULA, MARTIANS & ENSEMBLE.
WE'LL SING AND DANCE ALL NIGHT AND DAY,
AT THE BIGGEST BASH IN THE MILKY WAY.
WE PROMISE THERE'LL BE NO "MARS ATTACKS"
AT THE MARTIAN BALL!

NEBULA.

> HEY, HEY!
>
> COME ONE, COME ALL!
>
> AND BOOGIE WOOGIE
> BOOGIE
>
> AT THE MARTIAN BALL!

ALL OTHERS.

> HEY, HEY!
>
> COME ONE, COME ALL!
>
> AND BOOGIE WOOGIE
> BOOGIE
>
> AT THE MARTIAN BALL!

GROUP 1.

> HEY, HEY!
>
> COME ONE, COME ALL!
>
> AND BOOGIE WOOGIE
> BOOGIE
>
> AT THE MARTIAN BALL!

GROUP 2.

> HEY, HEY!
>
> COME ONE, COME ALL!
>
> AND BOOGIE WOOGIE
> BOOGIE
>
> AT THE MARTIAN BALL!

NEBULA. Thank you, everyone, for attending the annual Martian Ball! I am your host, Queen Nebula, and it is my pleasure to welcome our guests from several planets and solar systems. Did anyone fly all the way from Ursa Minor? That's a long trip...your arms must be tired! *(Cracks herself up.)* Now, I hope you didn't come across any Earthlings along the way!

ALL OTHERS. Ooh.

NEBULA. That would certainly spoil a Martian party! Well, my daughter, Alienne, promised me a dance, so let's get back to the festivities!

ALL.

> INVITE YOUR FRIENDS IN THE GALAXY,
> FROM JUPITER TO MERCURY,

FROM ANY STAR OR MOON OR SUN,
TO THE MARTIAN BALL!

NEBULA.

THERE'S JUST ONE RULE, OF WHICH WE'RE PROUD,

(Spoken in rhythm.)

AND THAT IS:

ALL. *(Spoken in rhythm.)*
NO EARTHLINGS ALLOWED!

(Sung.)

HUMANS AREN'T ANY FUN
AT THE MARTIAN BALL!

MARTY.

WEAR A SPACESUIT OR SHROUD,
SOMETHING YOU LOOK NICE IN.

MARSHA. *(Spoken in rhythm.)*
NICE OUTFIT!

MARTY. *(Spoken in rhythm.)*
THANKS!

NEBULA.

NO EARTHLINGS ALLOWED!

MARTY. *(Spoken in rhythm.)*
NOT EVEN NEIL DEGRASSE TYSON?

NEBULA. *(Spoken in rhythm.)*
NOT EVEN HIM!

ALL.

SO, SING AND DANCE FOR ALL YOU'RE WORTH,
UNLESS YOU COME FROM PLANET EARTH!
BUT OTHERWISE, BRING ANYONE
TO THE MARTIAN BALL!

*(**ALIENNE** exits the party.)*

GROUP 1.

> HEY, HEY!
>
> COME ONE, COME ALL!
>
> AND BOOGIE WOOGIE
> BOOGIE
>
> AT THE MARTIAN BALL!
>
> HEY, HEY!
>
> COME ONE, COME ALL!
>
> AND BOOGIE WOOGIE
> BOOGIE
>
> AT THE MARTIAN BALL!

GROUP 2.

> HEY, HEY!
>
> COME ONE, COME ALL!
>
> AND BOOGIE WOOGIE
> BOOGIE
>
> AT THE MARTIAN BALL!
>
> HEY, HEY!
>
> COME ONE, COME ALL!
>
> AND BOOGIE WOOGIE
> BOOGIE
>
> AT THE MARTIAN BALL!

ALL.

> IT'S THE MARTIAN BALL!
> COME ONE, COME ALL
> TO THE MARTIAN BALL!

NEBULA. Has anyone seen my daughter? She was here a moment ago. Alienne! Where is my little Martian?

[MUSIC NO 03A – MY LITTLE MARTIAN (REPRISE 2)]

MARTIANS & ENSEMBLE.

> MY LITTLE MARTIAN,
> LONG AGO AND FAR AWAY...
> MY LITTLE MARTIAN,
> THAT'S THE TALE WE'RE TELLING TODAY!

Scene Three: Alienne's Wish

COSMINA. Alienne, get out here! Your mother is looking for you! Are you hanging out in your pod again?

ALIENNE. Sorry, Cosmina, I was just looking out at all the beautiful stars and planets, dreaming about life on other worlds. *(Sigh.)*

COSMINA. That again? Girlfriend, you have got to get your head out of the stars! Your mother is going to kill you!

ALIENNE. Oh, I don't care about my stodgy old mother. I'm so bored being an all-knowing, perfect genius space creature.

COSMINA. I don't get it. Aren't you proud to be a Martian?

ALIENNE. Of course I am, Cosmina. It's just that…I want an adventure!

COSMINA. Alienne, don't take this the wrong way, but as your very best friend in the galaxy, I think it is my duty to tell you that…sometimes you act just like an Earthling!

(They both gasp.)

ALIENNE. What are you talking about?

COSMINA. Everyone knows that Martians are rational and logical, and we never let *emotions* get in our way. Only Earthlings are foolish enough to do that! I mean, even on other planets, they admire Martians and look down on Earthlings. It's just the way things are.

ALIENNE. Well, maybe it isn't the way they ought to be.

COSMINA. Do you really think you can change things after all these millennia?

ALIENNE. I don't know. I mean, we've heard the same old song and dance our whole lives.

COSMINA. Maybe it's time you hear it again.

[MUSIC NO. 04 – THE EARTHLING STOMP]

*(**ANCESTORS** enter and strike poses. **COSMINA**
indicates them as she says "father" or "fathers.")*

COSMINA. I mean, we've heard it from my father, from
your father, from their fathers... you know how it goes.

EARTHLINGS CAN BE SO IRRATIONAL,
BUILT IN SUCH A SIMPLE FASHION,
A LIVING THING CAN'T LIVE ON PASSION ALONE!

IT IS CLEAR THAT WE'RE SUPERIOR,
THEY CAN'T HELP BUT FEEL INFERIOR,
NOWHERE WILL YOU FIND A DREARIER DRONE!

ANYONE CAN SEE
THEY'RE NOT HALF AS BRIGHT AS WE,
SO LET THIS PLANET BE A HUMAN-FREE ZONE!

COSMINA & ANCESTORS.

EARTHLINGS HAVE A SINGULAR DEVOTION
TO A LIFE THAT'S MUDDLED WITH EMOTION!

COSMINA. *(Spoken in rhythm.)*
FOOLISH NOTION!

ANCESTORS.

HUMAN BEINGS MAKE MISTAKES A LOT,

COSMINA & ANCESTORS.

EV'RY EARTHLING FAILS AND BREAKS A LOT.
WE ALL KNOW...

COSMINA.

FOR GOODNESS SAKES...

COSMINA & ANCESTORS.

A LOT MORE!
LET THEM MAKE MISTAKES, HOWEVER, BE
PATIENT AS A SOUL COULD EVER BE.
SOMEDAY THEY MAY LEARN AS NEVER BEFORE!

COSMINA.
TILL THEN, THEY'LL RUST THEIR HEADS,
AND TRUST THEIR HEARTS INSTEAD!

COSMINA & ANCESTORS.
SO WHAT GOOD ARE THOSE HUMAN ANIMALS FOR?

(Dance break.)

What do humans do, anyway? They fall in love.

*(First **ANCESTOR** group freezes in goofy "love" pose.)*

They get dramatic about sports.

*(Second **ANCESTOR** group freezes in aggressive "spectator" pose.)*

They get upset over a bad haircut.

*(Third **ANCESTOR** group freezes in funny "crying" pose.)*

Frankly, I'd rather be a Martian!

COSMINA & ANCESTORS.
EARTHLINGS THINK THEY'RE COLORFUL AND CLEVER,
PROMISING TO LOVE OR HATE FOREVER!

COSMINA. *(Spoken in rhythm.)*
WHATEVER!

ANCESTOR GROUP 1.
HUMANS LACK OUR REASONED INTELLECT.

ANCESTOR GROUP 2.
HUMAN THOUGHT IS VAGUE AND INDIRECT.

ANCESTOR GROUP 3.
HUMAN SPEAKING TAKES THE INCORRECT TONE!

COSMINA & ANCESTORS.
> ANYONE CAN SEE,
> THEY'RE NOT HALF AS BRIGHT AS WE.
> SO LET THIS PLANET BE A HUMAN-FREE ZONE!
> LET THOSE EARTHLINGS KEEP TO THEIR OWN!

COSMINA. *(Spoken in rhythm.)*
> THAT'S WHAT THEY SAY!

And that is the way of the universe, Alienne. I know it stinks, but you better get used to it, my little Martian.

[MUSIC NO. 04A – MY LITTLE MARTIAN (REPRISE 3)]

COSMINA & ANCESTORS.
> MY LITTLE MARTIAN,
> LONG AGO AND FAR AWAY...
> MY LITTLE MARTIAN,
> THAT'S THE TALE WE'RE TELLING TODAY!

ALIENNE. I don't want to get used to it! I want to change it! In fact, I want to know what it's like to feel real feelings, to make mistakes, to wonder about things. Don't you?

COSMINA. I guess. I mean, it would be cool to learn stuff instead of being born knowing everything.

ALIENNE. Right! Cosmina, I know exactly what I want now.

COSMINA. You do? What?

ALIENNE. I want to be an Earthling!

[MUSIC NO. 05 – I WANNA BE A HUMAN]

COSMINA. Girl, you are one crazy Martian!

ALIENNE. I know...isn't it exciting?
> I WANNA BE A HUMAN BEING,
> I WANNA BE AN EARTHLING!
> I WANNA GO TO PLACES ONLY HUMANS CAN GO!

OH...

I WANNA SEE THE SIGHTS THEY'RE SEEING,
AND HEAR THE SONGS THEY'RE SINGING.
I WANNA KNOW THE THINGS NO MARTIAN
EVER SHOULD KNOW!

TO HAVE A HEART
PRONE TO GROWING AND BREAKING,
PASSIONS AND HEARTACHES.
I CAN START
JUST BY KNOWING I'M MAKING MISTAKES...
THAT'S ALL IT TAKES!
OH...

I WANNA BE A HUMAN BEING.
OH, WHY CAN NO ONE SEE?
A HUMAN BEING'S WHAT I WANNA BE!

COSMINA. But Alienne, you're a Martian. Why would you want to go and become human?

ALIENNE.

TO SEE MAPLE TREES AND MARIGOLDS,
TO WONDER WHAT THE FUTURE HOLDS,
AND ASK MYSELF, "WHAT MIGHT THAT FUTURE BRING?"
TO SEE MANATEES AND MYNAH BIRDS,
TO FEEL AND SHARE WITH MORE THAN WORDS.
TO KNOW A BIT, BUT NEVER QUITE KNOW EV'RYTHING...
EV'RYTHING!

I WANNA BE A HUMAN BEING.
OH, WHY CAN NO ONE SEE?
A HUMAN BEING'S WHAT I WANNA BE!

COSMINA. But how could you possibly transform? The only creature with the power to do that is Earthsula the Space Witch, and you don't want to mess with her!

ALIENNE. I'm not afraid of Earthsula. I'll do whatever it takes. She can send my soul to the Black Hole for all I care!

(**COSMINA** *gives up and exits.*)

ALIENNE.
I WANNA BE A HUMAN BEING.
OH, WHY CAN NO ONE SEE?
A HUMAN BEING'S WHAT I WANNA BE!

(Spoken in rhythm.)
I'M GONNA DO IT, YOU'LL SEE!

Scene Four: Tim's Wish

MARGO. Meanwhile, on planet Earth, a certain human guy was looking through his telescope, wondering about life on other worlds.

TIM. Wow... I can't believe what a clear night this is. The moon's so bright you could just reach out and catch it! Sprocket, check it out – a perfect view of Mars, the Red Planet!

SPROCKET. Yes, Tim... if it'll make you happy. *(He looks, then says, unenthusiastically.)* Ooh. Ah. I can hardly contain my enthusiasm. How do you humans do it?

TIM. Enough, wise guy. You know, I made you out of old hardware, and I could easily take you apart again.

SPROCKET. Whoa! No need to get your circuits crossed. I simply lack your human capacity for astonishment.

TIM. Remind me to program that into your hard drive during your next tune-up.

SPROCKET. Roger. "Program astonishment." Got it.

TIM. So, Sprocket... you think there are other creatures living on those planets up there?

SPROCKET. My database contains no evidence of carbon-based organisms in the galaxy, but you programmed me, and you could be wrong. After all, you are only human, and everyone knows humans make mistakes.

TIM. And what's so bad about that? It's how we learn.

SPROCKET. It just doesn't seem very efficient.

TIM. Well, I bet there's a creature out there who'd appreciate that I'm not exactly perfect.

SPROCKET. You're not perfect? This is news! I'll alert the media.

TIM. For your next tune-up, remind me to remove your sarcasm.

SPROCKET. "Remove Sarcasm." Got it.

TIM. You know, Sprocket, you're a cool robot and all, but sometimes I'd just rather be with something living.

SPROCKET. Like a puppy?

[MUSIC NO. 06 – I WANNA MEET A MARTIAN]

TIM. Sure. Or an alien life form. Something completely different, from... I don't know... Mars!

I WANNA MEET A MARTIAN CREATURE,
I WANNA MEET AN ALIEN!
I WANNA KNOW WHAT MAKES 'EM TICK,
BOTH INSIDE AND OUT.
OH...
I WANNA BE THEIR HUMAN TEACHER,
A MODERN-AGE PYGMALION.
I WANNA KNOW WHAT MARTIAN LIFE IS REALLY ABOUT!
OH, HOW I LONG
JUST TO STUDY ALL DAY
WHAT THEY THINK OR COMPREHEND.
I BELONG
WITH A BUDDY, A PLAYMATE, A FRIEND,
UNTIL THE END!
OH...
I WANNA MEET A MARTIAN CREATURE.
OH, WOULDN'T THAT BE NEAT?
A MARTIAN CREATURE'S WHAT I WANNA MEET!

SPROCKET. But there is no credible evidence of life on Mars.

TIM. I know. That only makes me wonder more!

SPROCKET. Humans!

TIM.

> ARE THEY REALLY GREEN WITH BUGGY EYES?
> ARE THEY TINY GUYS OR GIANT-SIZE?
> DO THEY HAVE AN ARM, A FLIPPER, OR A WING?
>
> ARE THEY REALLY CLEAN OR REALLY GROSS?
> ARE THEY SUPER-SHY OR GRANDIOSE?
> IF I MET ONE NOW, I KNOW I'D ASK THEM EV'RYTHING...
> EV'RYTHING!
>
> I WANNA MEET A MARTIAN CREATURE.
> OH, WOULDN'T THAT BE NEAT?
> A MARTIAN CREATURE'S WHAT I WANNA MEET!

ALIENNE.

ALIENNE	**TIM.**
I WANNA BE A	I WANNA MEET A
HUMAN BEING,	MARTIAN!
AND NOW IT'S CLEAR TO	IT'S CLEAR
ME –	TO ME –
A HUMAN BEING'S WHAT...	A MARTIAN CREATURE'S
	WHAT...
A HUMAN BEING'S WHAT...	A MARTIAN CREATURE'S
	WHAT...
	A MARTIAN CREATURE'S
A HUMAN BEING'S WHAT...	WHAT...
A HUMAN BEING'S WHAT...	WHAT...
I WANNA BE!	I WANNA SEE!
	IT'S DESTINY
I WANNA BE!	
	I GUARANTEE
I WANNA BE!	
EVENTUALLY,	I KNOW, EVENTUALLY,
IT'S GONNA HAPPEN TO	IT'S GONNA HAPPEN TO
ME!	ME!

Scene Five: The Deal

MARLIN. Of course, Earthsula the evil Space Witch had been listening in all the while. And she had an idea...

(**QUARK** *is napping and snoring.*)

EARTHSULA. Quark! Wake up and smell the cosmos!!

QUARK. Huh? What's going on?

EARTHSULA. You useless heap of space junk! My orbit is a mess! Why haven't you been working?

QUARK. Listen, your evilness, I'm having a bad millennium. Mercury is in retrograde, and my planets are completely out of alignment. Besides, you know I'm useless before my morning meteor shower.

EARTHSULA. What are you talking about? Get moving!

QUARK. Okay, but first I need to give my friend from Saturn a ring... get it? Saturn? A ring? "SATURN??"

(**EARTHSULA** *is unmoved.*)

Oh, come on. That's a good one.

EARTHSULA. We have some business to tend to.

QUARK. Okay, okay. So what's the word, oh great evil one?

EARTHSULA. A certain little Alienne from planet Mars wants to be a human! She actually wants to be an Earthling!

QUARK. Wait a second... "She" wants to? From planet Mars?

EARTHSULA. Yes.

QUARK. Are you sure you don't mean Venus?

EARTHSULA. No, I mean Mars. What are you getting at?

QUARK. Well, my cosmologist told me…"Men are from Mars, Women are from Venus!"

(**QUARK** *is cracking up again.*)

EARTHSULA. You don't understand… we are going to get another space soul for our little collection.

QUARK. You mean in the… yipes, I can hardly say it. In the, um, you know… the *Black Hole?*

EARTHSULA. You got it, my moronic space chum! Watch as I demonstrate my perfect spell:

[MUSIC NO. 07 – SPELL #1]

METEOR AND ASTEROID,
SEND THIS SOUL INTO THE VOID!
AS PLANETS ARE SPINNING AND GASES CHURN,
DISAPPEAR AND DON'T RETURN!

MERCURY, VENUS, EARTH AND MARS,
JUPITER, SATURN, URANUS AND NEPTUNE…
BUT NOT PLUTO!

Yup! Pluto's just a tiny dwarf planet! Awww… (*To audience.*) What? Too soon?

MERCURY, VENUS, EARTH AND MARS,
JUPITER, SATURN, URANUS AND NEPTUNE…
BUT NOT PLUTO!

EARTHSULA & QUARK. (*Spoken in rhythm.*)
COMET, VOMIT, PLPLPLP!

QUARK. Perfect as always, Earthsula. Not a trace of those Earthling mistakes in you, boss.

EARTHSULA. I know…I'm flawless! Oh, Alienne, you will soon be mine! Be careful what you wish for, my little Martian.

[MUSIC NO. 07A – MY LITTLE MARTIAN (REPRISE 4)]

MARTIANS & ENSEMBLE.
MY LITTLE MARTIAN,
LONG AGO AND FAR AWAY...
MY LITTLE MARTIAN,
THAT'S THE TALE WE'RE TELLING TODAY!

EARTHSULA. How dare you interrupt Earthsula, the Space Witch!

(**ALIENNE** *enters.*)

Ah, here you are, my little... *(Looks at audience.)* friend. So, Alienne, what do you want from old Earths?

QUARK. Yeah, what's your big wish, little Mars girl?

[MUSIC NO. 07B – I WANNA BE A HUMAN (A CAPPELLA)]

ALIENNE. *(A cappella.)*
I WANNA BE A HUMAN BEING,
I WANNA BE AN EARTHLING!

QUARK. For *realz*? Are you crazy? Why would anyone want to be a human?

EARTHSULA. Quit it, Quark. If little Alienne wants to be human, then she shall get her wish. You've come to the right place, my dear.

[MUSIC NO. 08 – SPACE WITCH]

'Cause when it comes to deal-making, nobody does it better than You-Know-Who. Sing it!

QUARK & ENSEMBLE.
EARTHSULA THE SPACE WITCH, BABY!
EARTHSULA THE SPACE WITCH, BABY!

MARTY. Hey, everybody, let's *all* sing this one.

MARSHA. When Earthsula makes sounds, everybody make them together. First, everyone, growl like a dog. *(Grr!)*

MARNIE. Great! Now roar like a lion. *(Roar!)*

MARGO. Good job! Now howl like a wolf. *(A-ooh!)* Excellent.

MARLIN. By Jupiter, I think they've got it.

EARTHSULA. It's about time. Can we get back to my song? Sing!

QUARK & ENSEMBLE.
EARTHSULA THE SPACE WITCH, BABY!
QUEEN OF THE GALAXY!

EARTHSULA.
SO YOU WANT A CHANGE?
YOU WANT SOMETHING NEW?
EARTHSULA WILL TELL YOU WHAT TO DO.

EARTHSULA.	**QUARK & ENSEMBLE.**
DO AS I SAY, AND YOU WILL GET THE THINGS YOU WANT IN SECONDS FLAT!	AH
WE CAN STRIKE A DEAL, AS LONG AS YOU REMEMBER THAT...	AH
I'M THE SPACE WITCH!	SPACE WITCH!

EARTHSULA.
MEAN AS ANY CREATURE CAN BE!

QUARK & ENSEMBLE.
EARTHSULA THE SPACE WITCH, BABY!

EARTHSULA.	**QUARK & ENSEMBLE.**
I'M THE SPACE WITCH!	SPACE WITCH!

EARTHSULA.
THERE IS NO ONE MEANER THAN ME!

QUARK & ENSEMBLE.
EARTHSULA THE SPACE WITCH, BABY!

EARTHSULA.

    OH, I CAN GROWL,

    I CAN ROAR,

    I CAN HOWL,

    I WANT MORE, MORE,
        MORE!
    I'M THE SPACE WITCH!

QUARK & ENSEMBLE.

    (Spoken in rhythm.)
    GRR!

    ROAR!

    A-OOH!

    (Sung.)
    SPACE WITCH!

EARTHSULA.

    QUEEN OF THE GALAXY!

QUARK & ENSEMBLE.

    EARTHSULA THE SPACE WITCH, BABY!

ALL.

    QUEEN OF THE GALAXY!

EARTHSULA.

    NOW, HERE'S THE DEAL:
    YOU'LL GET YOUR DREAM.
    CHANGE IS NOT AS HARD AS IT MAY SEEM.

EARTHSULA.

    BUT THERE'S A CATCH: I
        GIVE YOU EV'RYTHING
        YOU DREAMED ABOUT,
        BUT THEN I
    TAKE AWAY YOUR
        MARTIAN BRAINS
        AND BOTH* OF YOUR
        ANTENNAE!
    'CAUSE I'M THE
        SPACE WITCH!

QUARK & ENSEMBLE.

    AH

    AH

    SPACE WITCH!

---

*If Alienne's costume has more than two antennae, licensees may replace
BOTH with ALL.

EARTHSULA.

MEAN AS ANY CREATURE CAN BE!

QUARK & ENSEMBLE.

EARTHSULA THE SPACE WITCH, BABY!

EARTHSULA.	**QUARK & ENSEMBLE.**
I'M THE SPACE WITCH!	SPACE WITCH!
AIN'T NOBODY MEANER	
THAN ME!	

QUARK & ENSEMBLE.

EARTHSULA THE SPACE WITCH, BABY!

EARTHSULA.	**QUARK & ENSEMBLE.**
OH, I CAN GROWL,	*(Spoken in rhythm.)*
	GRR!
I CAN ROAR,	
	ROAR!
I CAN HOWL,	
	A-OOH!
I WANT MORE, MORE,	
MORE!	*(Sung.)*
I'M THE SPACE WITCH!	SPACE WITCH!

EARTHSULA.

QUEEN OF THE GALAXY!

QUARK & ENSEMBLE.

EARTHSULA THE SPACE WITCH, BABY!

ALL.

QUEEN OF THE GALAXY!

EARTHSULA.

BUT WAIT! THERE'S MORE –
ONE PRICE TO PAY:

ALL.

YOU'LL ONLY GET YOUR WISH FOR JUST ONE DAY.

EARTHSULA.   **QUARK & ENSEMBLE.**

    I'M GIVING YOU MY FINAL   AH
        WARNING, SO YOU
        BETTER READ MY LIPS:
    YOU HAD BEST RETURN   AH
        BEFORE TOMORROW'S
        BIG ECLIPSE!

EARTHSULA.

    IF NOT, I'LL TAKE CONTROL,
    AND CLAIM YOUR MARTIAN SOUL.

ALL.

    YOU'LL TAKE YOUR FINAL STROLL
    INTO THE BIG BLACK HOLE!

EARTHSULA.   **QUARK & ENSEMBLE.**

    OH, I'M THE SPACE WITCH!   SPACE WITCH!
    MEAN AS ANY CREATURE
        CAN BE!

QUARK & ENSEMBLE.

    EARTHSULA THE SPACE WITCH, BABY!

EARTHSULA.   **QUARK & ENSEMBLE.**

    I'M THE SPACE WITCH!   SPACE WITCH!
    AIN'T NOBODY MEANER
        THAN ME!

QUARK & ENSEMBLE.

    EARTHSULA THE SPACE WITCH, BABY!

EARTHSULA.   **QUARK & ENSEMBLE.**

    OH, I CAN GROWL,   *(Spoken in rhythm.)*
        GRR!

    I CAN ROAR,

        ROAR!

    I CAN HOWL,

        A-OOH!

EARTHSULA.

I WANT MORE, MORE, MORE!

EARTHSULA.	**QUARK & ENSEMBLE.**
I'M THE SPACE WITCH!	SPACE WITCH!
QUEEN OF THE GALAXY!	

QUARK & ENSEMBLE.

EARTHSULA THE SPACE WITCH, BABY!

ALL.

QUEEN OF THE GALAXY!

QUARK. Okay, Alienne, here she goes! But remember, you have to be back before the Solar Eclipse, or you'll be sucked into the Black Hole!

ALIENNE. I'll remember!

[MUSIC NO. 09 – SPELL #2]

EARTHSULA.

POWERS OF SPACE, FOR ALL YOU'RE WORTH,
MAKE THIS CREATURE FIT FOR EARTH!
AS COMETS AND GALAXIES SWIRL AND STORM,
CHANGE HER INTO HUMAN FORM!

MERCURY, VENUS, EARTH AND MARS,
JUPITER, SATURN, URANUS AND NEPTUNE...
BUT NOT PLUTO!

EARTHSULA, QUARK & ENSEMBLE. *(Spoken in rhythm.)*
COMET, VOMIT, PLPLPLP!

*(**ALIENNE** is magically transformed.)*

ALIENNE. Am I...am I human?

EARTHSULA. Yeah, yeah, queen for a day. You got your wish, little girl.

ALIENNE. And I can communicate with Earthlings?

EARTHSULA. Sure. No problem.

QUARK. *(Mystified.)* For some reason, we've all been speaking English already.

EARTHSULA. *(To the audience.)* Don't think too hard, or the whole story falls apart.

ALIENNE. So, how do I get to Earth?

EARTHSULA. Beats me. That wasn't part of the deal. Guess you're on your own, kid.

ALIENNE. But that's not fair.

EARTHSULA. Who ever said I was fair?

[MUSIC NO. 10 – SPACE WITCH (REPRISE)]

EARTHSULA.	**QUARK & ENSEMBLE.**
I'M THE SPACE WITCH! ALL MY PLANS ARE SORTA PERVERSE!	SPACE WITCH!
	EARTHSULA THE SPACE WITCH, BABY!
I'M THE SPACE WITCH! TRY AN' NAME ME ANYONE WORSE!	SPACE WITCH!
	EARTHSULA THE SPACE WITCH, BABY!
OH, I CAN THRILL!	*(Spoken in rhythm.)* THRILL!
I CAN CHILL!	
	CHILL!
I CAN KILL!	**QUARK.** *(Spoken in rhythm.)* KILL?
I WON'T QUIT UNTIL I'M THE SPACE WITCH! QUEEN OF THE UNIVERSE!	**QUARK & ENSEMBLE.** SPACE WITCH!
	EARTHSULA THE SPACE WITCH, BABY!
QUEEN OF THE UNIVERSE!	QUEEN OF THE UNIVERSE!

Scene Six: The Meeting

MARTY. So, Alienne was transformed. She needed to get to Earth fast, so she "borrowed" her mother's best space pod.

MARSHA. But she was a human driver, so she had a bit of trouble with the landing.

MARNIE. And she just happened to crash on the front lawn of our friend, Tim.

SPROCKET. A-hem!

MARGO. And his robot buddy, Sprocket.

SPROCKET. Thank you.

MARLIN. Now, that crash must have made a lot of noise, so on the count of three, let's all yell "CRASH!" as loud as we can. Ready? 1-2-3...

MARTIANS & AUDIENCE. CRASH!

TIM. Whoa, Sprocket, did you hear that?

SPROCKET. Does Jupiter have moons? Of course I heard it!

TIM. We really have to do something about that sarcasm.

(**TIM** *looks up.*)

Hey, look...it's a spaceship! Sprocket, my wish came true... it's my little Martian!

[MUSIC NO. 10A – MY LITTLE MARTIAN (REPRISE 5)]

MARTIANS & ENSEMBLE.
MY LITTLE MARTIAN,
LONG AGO AND FAR AWAY...
MY LITTLE MARTIAN,
THAT'S THE TALE WE'RE TELLING TODAY!

(**ALIENNE** *enters, fully humanized.*)

SPROCKET. She looks pretty earth-bound to me.

ALIENNE. Excuse me... maybe you could help me. I'm a little lost.

TIM. *(Excited.)* Why? Are you here from, I don't know, another planet or something?

ALIENNE. Ye... I mean, no, of course not. I was just flying around in my... um... Earth jet. I mean, people pod. I mean, uh, aviational aeronautic human transport.

SPROCKET. You mean an airplane?

ALIENNE. Yes, my airplane.

TIM. *(Disappointed.)* Oh, right – a mini-plane. It sure looked like a spacecraft.

ALIENNE. Well, it's a crazy new design.

TIM. I've never seen anything like it. Like a VZ-9 Avrocar, but way cooler. Are you all right?

ALIENNE. Yes.

(**ALIENNE** *starts to faint.*)

No.

(She sits.)

It was just a tiny little accident, that's all.

SPROCKET. Hmmph. Accidents. Obviously human.

TIM. Do you need anything? A glass of water? Some gum? I have Orbit or Eclipse.

ALIENNE. No, thanks. I'm perfectly content just the way I am.

TIM. Good. Hey, that was some flight! Where'd you learn how to fly?

ALIENNE. I never *learned*, I just... I mean... I took a lot of lessons.

TIM. That's cool. I've studied everything there is to know about aircraft. And space. I love learning about new things.

ALIENNE. Me too. Lucky I met you.

[MUSIC NO. 11 – CATCH THE MOON]

TIM. I'm Tim, and this is my buddy, Sprocket.

SPROCKET. Pleasure to make your acquaintance.

ALIENNE.

I'M ALIENNE.
I'M A LITTLE UNSURE OF WHAT TO DO...
HERE EV'RYTHING'S SO NEW,
I DON'T KNOW WHERE TO BEGIN.

TIM.

WELL, ALIENNE,
YOU'RE IN LUCK, 'CAUSE I'M HERE TO LEND A HAND.
IT LOOKS LIKE WHEN YOU LANDED,
YOU DESTABILIZED YOUR FIN.

HEY, MAYBE WE CAN TRY
TO FIX IT UP NOW, YOU AND ME.
I HAPPEN TO BE FREE FOR THE AFTERNOON.

ALIENNE. Me, too!

TIM.

AND ONCE WE MAKE IT FLY,
WE'LL SEE HOW FAR THIS BABY GOES.
AND THEN, WHO KNOWS?
WE MIGHT CATCH THE MOON!

ALIENNE. Catch the moon?

SPROCKET. It's a metaphor. A figure of speech in which a term or phrase is applied to something to which it is not literally applicable in order to suggest a resemblance, as in "Tim's feet are stink-bombs."

TIM. Thanks, Sprocket. "Catch the moon" means to reach out and grab something you always dreamed about. To see something you've never seen.

ALIENNE. Like something from another world?

TIM. Yeah, like that.

ALIENNE. So it means to wish for something impossible, even if it doesn't make any sense.

TIM. I guess it does. Come on... let's get to work.

MARTY. So, they spent some time repairing the pod... uh, *plane.*

MARSHA. Finally, just as the sun was setting, they were ready for a test run.

TIM. I can't believe you know how to fly! Can we try it?

ALIENNE. Of course. It's easy!

SPROCKET. Danger! Danger! Tim has never navigated an aeronautic human transport before.

ALIENNE. Yeah, but have you ever flown a plane?

TIM. No time like the present! You coming, Sprocket?

SPROCKET. No, thanks. I'm staying here on the ground, where no humans can accidentally dent my hardware.

TIM. Okay, we'll see you later!

MARTIANS & ENSEMBLE.
>AND SO THEY FLEW,
>FLOATING GRACEFULLY OVER FIELDS AND HILLS,
>ENJOYING ALL THE THRILLS
>OF FINDING NEW WORLDS TO EXPLORE.

ALIENNE.

> DREAMS DO COME TRUE,
> WHEN YOUR CRAZIEST FEELINGS ARE SET FREE.

TIM.

> THAT'S WHEN YOU'RE BOUND TO SEE
> THE THINGS YOU'VE NEVER SEEN BEFORE.

TIM & ALIENNE.

> AND EV'RY TINY STAR'S
> A SPARKLING DIAMOND IN THE SKY
> AS, WEIGHTLESSLY, WE FLY LIKE A TOY BALLOON.
>
> THE PLANETS NEAR AND FAR
> ARE PAPER LANTERNS FLOATING BY,
> AND YOU AND I...
> WE CAN CATCH THE MOON!

TIM.

> I USED TO SOAR THROUGH SPACE
> IN MY IMAGINATION
> WHEN I WAS SMALL,
> BUT THAT WAS JUST PRETEND.

ALIENNE.

> HERE IN THIS MAGIC PLACE,
> I FEEL SUCH INSPIRATION!

ALIENNE & TIM.

> AND BEST OF ALL,
> I MADE A BRAND-NEW FRIEND.

TIM. You know, I think we're a little lost. We must have missed a turn.

ALIENNE. That's okay. This is fun!

TIM. My GPS doesn't even recognize this area. It's uncharted!

ALIENNE. So our mistake helped us find something new! Amazing.

ALL.
> AND EV'RY TINY STAR'S
> A SPARKLING DIAMOND IN THE SKY
> AS, WEIGHTLESSLY, WE FLY LIKE A TOY BALLOON.
>
> THE PLANETS NEAR AND FAR
> ARE PAPER LANTERNS FLOATING BY,
> AND THE GALAXY,
> IN ALL ITS MAJESTY,
> IS SAYING, "LOOK AND SEE –
> YOU CAN CATCH THE MOON!"

GROUP 1.
> WE CAN CATCH...

GROUP 2.
> WE CAN CATCH...

GROUP 3.
> WE CAN CATCH...

ALL.
> THE MOON!

Scene Seven: The Reaction

MARNIE. Meanwhile, back on the Red Planet…

NEBULA. *(Entering.)* Alienne? I can't find that Martian anywhere! I've tried to contact her, but her antennae seem to be malfunctioning. That girl is so headstrong – she could be anywhere by now.

[MUSIC NO. 12 –ALIENNE]

My stars, things were so much easier when she was little.

ALIENNE, ALIENNE,
CAN YOU EVEN REMEMBER WHEN
I SPOKE AND YOU CALMLY CONSENTED?

WELL, I CAN, NOW AND THEN,
AND I THINK OF YOU, ALIENNE,
SO SIMPLE AND PURE AND CONTENTED.

BUT YOU GREW.
I GUESS YOU KNEW
THAT THERE WAS NOTHING I COULD DO,
FOR GROWING UP CAN'T BE PREVENTED.

SO YOU FLEW VERY FAR,
AND I'M NOT SURE JUST WHERE YOU ARE,
BUT I'LL COME AND FIND YOU,
TO FIRMLY REMIND YOU
THAT YOU'LL BE MY MARTIAN AGAIN,
ALIENNE.

*(**COSMINA** enters, sees **NEBULA**, and tries to discreetly exit.)*

Cosmina!

COSMINA. Yes, Your Majesty.

NEBULA. Have you seen Alienne?

COSMINA. No, ma'am. Not since the ball.

NEBULA. Do you know where she is?

COSMINA. Oh, gosh. Uh... I couldn't say.

NEBULA. Hmm. I wonder where she may be.

COSMINA. You *wonder*?

NEBULA. Yes, I wonder. This is perplexing. I am not accustomed to wondering about things... I've always known everything before! *(She smiles.)* It's a bit refreshing, actually.

COSMINA. I thought only Earthlings wondered.

NEBULA. *(Making excuses.)* Well, I actually...you see, I wasn't really... *(Suddenly angry.)* Now, see here! I will not be compared to an Earthling! This is precisely why we must find Alienne, and soon. I will not tolerate any more of this *wondering* business, not while I am Queen of Mars. So we will find Alienne and bring her home. Do you hear me?

COSMINA. Yes, Your Majesty.

NEBULA. We'll search all of Mars! I'll go east, you go west, and we'll meet back here in an hour.

COSMINA. One hour? For the whole planet?

NEBULA. No time to waste!

NEBULA.	**COSMINA.**
ALIENNE, ALIENNE,	ALIENNE!
YOU WILL NOT DISOBEY AGAIN!	I LIED
NO, I'LL COME AND GET YOU,	FOR YOU!
IT'S MORE THAN A THREAT,	NOW WHAT CAN I DO?
YOU'LL SEE, I'LL NEVER LET YOU SLIP OUT OF MY SIGHT AGAIN...	YOU'LL SEE, SHE'LL NEVER LET YOU SLIP OUT OF HER SIGHT AGAIN...

COSMINA. Girl, you owe me!

NEBULA.

ALIENNE!

COSMINA.

ALIENNE!

(**NEBULA** *and* **COSMINA** *exit.*)

MARGO. *(To audience.)* You think that was dramatic? You should see how Earthsula reacted.

EARTHSULA. *(Entering.)* Curses! That little brat is having the time of her Martian life! I will not tolerate a soul in my custody *enjoying* herself! Quark!

(**QUARK** *enters, sleepily.*)

QUARK. What could possibly be important enough to interrupt my beauty rest?

EARTHSULA. We are going to Earth, you numbskull.

QUARK. Today? But...what should I wear? My baby-blue travel suit? My burgundy blazer? And who has time to pack?

EARTHSULA. There will be no packing! We won't be staying long... just long enough for that solar eclipse to overshadow all of little Alienne's dreams.

QUARK. But boss, if we go to Earth, they're sure to recognize we're extraterrestrial! You know... *(Poking his finger towards her.)* "ET phone home."

(**EARTHSULA** *smacks his hand away.*)

EARTHSULA. Cut that out.

QUARK. *(In a funny voice.)* "Ouch."

EARTHSULA. We're going to be disguised. I'm going to become part human, so no one will realize that I'm Evil Queen of the Galaxy.

QUARK. Maybe you should go as you are, and they'll just think you're a professional wrestler.

EARTHSULA. Watch it, buster, or I'll grind you to space dust. Now, you are going to be my darling pet kitty.

QUARK. But I'm allergic to cat fur!

EARTHSULA. Deal with it.

[MUSIC NO. 13 – SPELL #3]

GALAXIES THAT SWIRL AND STORM,
CHANGE ME INTO HUMAN FORM!
I BECKON THE UNIVERSE, MAKE ME SWITCH
TO PARTLY HUMAN, PARTLY WITCH.
(Spoken in rhythm.)
WHILE YOU'RE AT IT, MAKE THIS BRAT
A FURRY LITTLE STINKIN' CAT.

QUARK. *(Spoken in rhythm.)*
THANKS, BOSS.

EARTHSULA. *(Spoken in rhythm.)*
DON'T MENTION IT.
(Sung.)
THERE'S ANOTHER THING AS WELL:
ADD A LITTLE MEMORY SPELL
SO ALIENNE WON'T BE ALLOWED TO SEE
THIS HUMAN STRANGER'S REALLY ME!
(Spoken in rhythm.)
IS THAT EV'RYTHING?

QUARK. *(Spoken in rhythm.)*
THAT ABOUT COVERS IT, BOSS.

EARTHSULA. *(Spoken in rhythm.)*
GOOD!
(Sung.)
MERCURY, VENUS, EARTH AND MARS,
JUPITER, SATURN, URANUS AND NEPTUNE...
BUT NOT PLUTO.

EARTHSULA, QUARK, MARTIANS & ENSEMBLE.
(*Spoken in rhythm.*)
COMET, VOMIT, PLPLPLP!

EARTHSULA. HAH!

(**EARTHSULA** *and* **QUARK** *realize they haven't changed at all.*)

The spell will take effect soon enough. Now, let's get to Earth and quick. You'll see who's boss now, my little Martian!

[MUSIC NO. 13A – MY LITTLE MARTIAN (REPRISE 6)]

(**EARTHSULA** *groans as she realizes she's said it again.*)

MARTIANS & ENSEMBLE.
MY LITTLE MARTIAN,
LONG AGO AND FAR AWAY...
MY LITTLE MARTIAN,
THAT'S THE TALE WE'RE TELLING TODAY!

(**COSMINA** *enters, looking worried.* **NEBULA** *then enters briskly.*)

NEBULA. Cosmina! Right on time. Did you find Alienne?

COSMINA. No, ma'am.

NEBULA. Nor did I. And you looked everywhere?

COSMINA. (*Obviously lying.*) Yes, ma'am.

NEBULA. The entire western hemisphere?

COSMINA. (*Agonizing.*) Yes, ma'am.

NEBULA. Not a stone unturned?

COSMINA. No, ma'am.

NEBULA. Are you sure you –

COSMINA. *(Finally breaking.)* Oh, all right! I lied, okay? I lied to a queen! I know where Alienne is. *(Suddenly very fast.)* She had this crazy idea to become a human. She kept saying *(Singing.)* "I Wanna Be a Human Being," and I said, "But Alienne, the only creature with the power to do that is Earthsula, the Space Witch, and you don't wanna mess with her," and she said, "I'm not afraid of her. I'll do whatever it takes. She can send my soul to the Black Hole for all I care!" And then she started singing again, so I just threw up my hands and walked away and –

NEBULA. COSMINA!

COSMINA. Yes, ma'am.

NEBULA. Where is she?

COSMINA. She borrowed your space pod and flew to Earth!

NEBULA. Earth? Oh no! This is terrible. If I could just see her again, I'd feel so much better.

COSMINA. You'd *feel* better? Your Majesty, excuse me for saying so, but... having feelings? That's all Alienne ever wanted.

NEBULA. I guess it was. I've got to find Alienne and tell her she was right! *(Suddenly motivated.)* Cosmina, we're going to Earth!

COSMINA. We can take my pod!

NEBULA. Mama's coming to save you, my little Martian!

[MUSIC NO. 13B – MY LITTLE MARTIAN (REPRISE 7)]

MARTIANS & ENSEMBLE.
MY LITTLE MARTIAN,
LONG AGO AND FAR AWAY...
MY LITTLE MARTIAN,
THAT'S THE TALE WE'RE TELLING TODAY!

Scene Eight: The Confrontation

TIM. So, that's when I first started studying outer space.

ALIENNE. Wow, I can't believe how much you know. And you had to learn it all? I mean, you didn't just know it all to begin with?

TIM. What do you mean? Was I born knowing everything? Now, that would be strange, wouldn't it?

ALIENNE. Yeah, I guess it would.

TIM. Strange, but amazing.

ALIENNE. Oh, I don't know. It wasn't so great.

TIM. What's that?

ALIENNE. Oh, nothing.

TIM. Alienne, you sure are different from everybody around here. Where did you say you were from again?

ALIENNE. France.

TIM. Right. Hey, do you have any idea what time it is?

ALIENNE. No, I don't. But I'm sure I've got plenty of time.

MARLIN. Of course, the Solar Eclipse was fast approaching...

[MUSIC NO. 14 – THE SOLAR ECLIPSE, PART 1]*

MARTIANS & ENSEMBLE (GROUP 2).	**MARTIANS & ENSEMBLE (GROUP 3).**
TICK TOCK, TICK TOCK, TICK TOCK, TICK TOCK.	BUM BUM BUM BUMP BU-DUM
TICK TOCK, TICK TOCK, TICK TOCK, TICK TOCK.	BUM BUM BUM BUMP BU-DUM

---

*An alternate simplified two-part harmony version is also available.

GROUP 1.	GROUP 2.	GROUP 3.
TIME KEEPS	TICK TOCK,	BUM
PASSING,	TICK TOCK,	BUM
NO ONE	TICK TOCK,	BUM BUMP
SEEMS TO	TICK TOCK.	BU-DU
CARE.	TICK TOCK,	BUM
	TICK TOCK,	BUM
	TICK TOCK,	BUM BUMP
	TICK TOCK.	BU-DUM
SHADOWS	TICK TOCK,	BUM
THREATEN,	TICK TOCK,	BUM
DANGER'S IN	TICK TOCK,	BUM BUMP
THE	TICK TOCK.	BU-DUM
AIR!	TICK TOCK,	BUM
	TICK TOCK,	BUM
	TICK TOCK.	BUM BUMP

MARTIANS & ENSEMBLE.
TIME DRIFTS AWAY THROUGHOUT THE DAY,
SEE HOW IT SLOWLY SLIPS.
SO BEWARE THE SOLAR

GROUP 1.	GROUP 2.	GROUP 3.
ECLIPSE...	TICK TOCK,	BUM
	TICK TOCK,	BUM
	TICK TOCK,	BUM BUMP
	TICK TOCK.	BU-DUM
ECLIPSE...	TICK TOCK,	BUM
	TICK TOCK,	BUM
	TICK TOCK,	BUM BUMP
	TICK TOCK.	BU-DUM
ECLIPSE...	TICK TOCK,	BUM
	TICK TOCK,	BUM
	TICK TOCK,	BUM BUMP
	TICK TOCK.	BU-DUM
ECLIPSE!	ECLIPSE!	ECLIPSE!

MARTY. Suddenly, there was an awful crash.

MARTIANS. 1-2-3...

MARTIANS & AUDIENCE. CRASH!

QUARK. Holy Mercury! Did you have to drive so fast? I think I got whiplash.

EARTHSULA. Well, if you hadn't made me stop at Alpha Centauri for solar snacks, I could have gotten us here a lot sooner!

QUARK. Listen, I'm not the one who insisted on taking the Milky Way… everyone knows the Thruway is faster!

EARTHSULA. Listen, you, I've had about enough of your wise talk!

TIM. Hey, are you all right over there?

EARTHSULA. *(Sweet voice.)* Oh, dear me, what shall we do?

TIM. Uh…Hi, I'm Tim and this is Alienne. What's the problem?

EARTHSULA. Hi, Timsy-wimsy. I'm Astronella von Orbit, and this is my kitty, Snuffles.

(**EARTHSULA** *elbows* **QUARK.**)

QUARK. Meow.

EARTHSULA. We seem to have kwashed our wittle pwane. Whatever shall we do? We'd wuv it if you'd help.

QUARK. *(To* **EARTHSULA,** *mocking her.)* Oh, we kwashed our pwane. It's weewee bwoken.

EARTHSULA. *(To* **QUARK.***)* Zip it! *(To* **TIM.***)* So, do you think you could help my kitty and me?

(Nudges **QUARK** *to act cute.)*

QUARK. Meow. Meow. *(Sneezes.)* I should have brought my inhaler.

TIM. Sure, I guess we could all try to repair your plane.

ALIENNE. Gee, I really should keep an eye on the clock.

EARTHSULA. But what will I do? How will I get home? I need your help.

ALIENNE. Oh, all right. I mean, we already fixed one plane, why not fix two?

TIM. Exactly. But we should hurry... this could take a while.

EARTHSULA. Oh, that's no problem. I've got all day.

QUARK. Oh, come on...my allergy medicine only lasts four hours. *(Sneezes.)*

EARTHSULA. Can it, kitty.

[MUSIC NO. 14A – THE SOLAR ECLIPSE, PART 2]

MARTIANS & ENSEMBLE (GROUP 2).	MARTIANS & ENSEMBLE (GROUP 3).
TICK TOCK, TICK TOCK, TICK TOCK, TICK TOCK.	BUM BUM BUM BUMP BU-DUM
TICK TOCK, TICK TOCK, TICK TOCK, TICK TOCK.	BUM BUM BUM BUMP BU-DUM

GROUP 1.	GROUP 2.	GROUP 3.
SOMETHING'S	TICK TOCK,	BUM
CHANGING	TICK TOCK,	BUM
IN THE	TICK TOCK,	BUM BUMP
ATMO-	TICK TOCK.	BU-DUM
-SPHERE.	TICK TOCK,	BUM
	TICK TOCK,	BUM
	TICK TOCK,	BUM BUMP
	TICK TOCK.	BU-DUM
THE SPACE	TICK TOCK,	BUM
WITCH	TICK TOCK,	BUM
KNOWS	TICK TOCK,	BUM BUMP
THE END IS	TICK TOCK.	BU-DUM
DRAWING		
NEAR.	TICK TOCK,	BUM
	TICK TOCK,	BUM
	TICK TOCK.	BUM BUMP

MARTIANS & ENSEMBLE.
WHY CAN'T THEY SEE THAT VICTORY
IS AT HER FINGERTIPS?
DON'T IGNORE THE SOLAR

GROUP 1.	GROUP 2.	GROUP 3.
ECLIPSE...	TICK TOCK,	BUM
	TICK TOCK,	BUM
	TICK TOCK,	BUM BUMP
	TICK TOCK.	BU-DUM
ECLIPSE...	TICK TOCK,	BUM
	TICK TOCK,	BUM
	TICK TOCK,	BUM BUMP
	TICK TOCK.	BU-DUM
ECLIPSE...	TICK TOCK,	BUM
	TICK TOCK,	BUM
	TICK TOCK,	BUM BUMP
	TICK TOCK.	BU-DUM
ECLIPSE!	ECLIPSE!	ECLIPSE!

TIM. Almost done! Just a few more touches, and –

ALIENNE. Hey, is it me, or is it getting dark in here?

QUARK. Yeah, who's puttin' out the lights?

EARTHSULA. 3-2-1...

(Removes disguise.)

HA!! THE SOLAR ECLIPSE!!

ALIENNE. Earthsula?

EARTHSULA. You got it, sweetheart!

TIM. What? What's going on?

ALIENNE. It's the Solar Eclipse! We ran out of time!

MARSHA. Just then, Queen Nebula's pod crashed.

MARTIANS. 1-2-3...

MARTIANS & AUDIENCE. CRASH!

QUARK. Doesn't anyone around here know how to properly land a space pod?

(**NEBULA** *suddenly enters.*)

NEBULA. Alienne? Is that you?

ALIENNE. Mama! Yes, it's me!

NEBULA. Oh, my Martian girl!

TIM. Wait a minute... Alienne, you're a Martian?

ALIENNE. Yes, I am. I mean, I was, but Earthsula turned me into a human.

EARTHSULA. And now I'm turning you into a memory. Your soul is mine, sister.

NEBULA. Wait! Earthsula...

(**ALL** *freeze.*)

Take me instead.

OTHERS. What?

NEBULA. Take my soul instead. I want to save Alienne because she's my daughter and...I love her.

(**ALL** *gasp.*)

ALIENNE. But Mama, we're Martians. We don't let emotions get in our way.

NEBULA. Then what's the point of being here, Alienne? When you were missing...

[MUSIC NO. 15 – ALIENNE (REPRISE)]

I discovered that having feelings, even bad feelings, is what makes you alive.

ALIENNE, ALIENNE,
I WAS ANGRY AND HURT, AND THEN
I LEARNED THAT I COULD FEEL A FEELING.

IT WAS STRANGE, QUITE A CHANGE,
BUT I SOON LEARNED TO REARRANGE
EMOTIONS I HAD BEEN CONCEALING.
THEY WERE NEW, BUT THEY WERE TRUE,
AND IT WAS ALL BECAUSE OF YOU
THAT I FOUND A PATHWAY TO HEALING.
SO I'M HERE, QUITE SINCERE,
AS I STEP UP TO VOLUNTEER
TO SHOW MY LOVE FOR YOU,
'CAUSE I DO ADORE YOU,
AND I WON'T IGNORE YOU AGAIN,
ALIENNE.

Thank you, Alienne. You taught me to feel.

ALL.

ALIENNE.

NEBULA. So, Earthsula, I want you to spare my daughter and send me to the Black Hole instead.

EARTHSULA. Whatever. I'll take a queen over a princess any day. Here goes:

[MUSIC NO. 16 – SPELL #4]

METEOR AND ASTEROID,
SEND THIS SOUL INTO THE VOID!
AS PLANETS ARE SPINNING AND GASES CHURN,
DISAPPEAR AND DON'T RETURN!
MERCURY, MARS, VENUS...

(Realizes she's mistaken.)

No, wait, it's...

MERCURY, SATURN, VENUS...

No...

MERCURY, PLUTO...

Pluto? Pluto's not even a planet! I...I can't remember.

QUARK. Hey boss, you're still part human, remember? And everyone knows...humans make mistakes!

EARTHSULA. No, this can't be! If I say the words wrong, the spell is automatically...

ALL. REVERSED!

EARTHSULA. Which means I get sent into the Black Hole!

QUARK. And all the souls you've sent there are set free!

[MUSIC NO. 16A – EARTHSULA'S END]

EARTHSULA. Nooo!!

> (**EARTHSULA** *is sucked into the Black Hole. Sound effects, lighting, and general chaos.*)

ALIENNE. Hey, my antennae are back!

TIM. So, Alienne, you're not an Earthling?

ALIENNE. No, I'm not.

TIM. Wow.

ALIENNE. Before you say anything,

[MUSIC NO. 17 – FINALE: BE WHO YOU ARE]

just let me explain.

I DIDN'T WANT TO BE A MARTIAN,
I CHANGED ALL THAT I APPEARED TO BE.
I HURT SOMEONE WHO WAS DEAR TO ME,
ALL FOR SOME FOOLISH FLING.
(Spoken in rhythm.)
SORRY, MOM. AND TIM...
(Sung.)
I'M SORRY I LIED TO YOU.
MAYBE I TRIED TO DO
MORE THAN I COULD SWING.
I SPOILED A WONDERFUL NIGHT...

TIM. *(Spoken in rhythm.)*
ALIENNE, IT'S ALL RIGHT.
(Sung.)
AND I WOULDN'T CHANGE A THING.

ALIENNE. You wouldn't?

TIM. No. I always wanted to meet a real alien, and now I have.

ALIENNE. And I always wanted to know what it's like to be a human, and now I do!

QUARK. Well, I never cared to know what it's like to be a cat, but I know that anyway.

ALIENNE. So, we can still be friends?

TIM. Of course!

ALIENNE. But I'm back to being a Martian.

TIM. So what?
BE WHO YOU ARE...
BE WHATEVER IT IS THAT YOU WERE BORN TO BE.
CAN'T YOU SEE
THAT YOU'RE THE ONE AND ONLY YOU?
BE WHO YOU ARE...
IN EV'RYTHING YOU DO!
LET YOUR SPIRIT SOAR
AS YOU FOLLOW YOUR OWN STAR.
BE WHO YOU ARE.

NEBULA. You know, Tim, you're awfully smart...for a *human.*

ALIENNE. Mother!

NEBULA. Oh, I'm just kidding.
I'VE BEEN A LITTLE ROUGH ON EARTHLINGS.
I THOUGHT FEELINGS ONLY MAKE YOU STRANGE.
TURNS OUT, MAKING A MISTAKE CAN CHANGE
YOU IN A USEFUL WAY.

ALIENNE & COSMINA.
> SO NOW, INSTEAD OF BERATING
> AND JUDGING AND HATING
> THOSE EARTHLINGS FAR AWAY,
> CAN WE WELCOME THEM ALL
> TO A NEW MARTIAN BALL?

NEBULA. *(Spoken in rhythm.)*
> LET'S HAVE ONE HERE, TODAY!

ALIENNE. Really?

NEBULA. Sure... a new Martian Ball. This time, bring all the humans you like! *(Indicating* **COSMINA, SPROCKET** *and* **QUARK.***)* And all the best friends, and all the robots, and all the... Quark, what exactly *are* you?

QUARK. I am special and unique.

ALIENNE. Well, whatever you are...you're invited.

NEBULA, ALIENNE & COSMINA.
> COME AS YOU ARE...
> BE WHATEVER IT IS THAT YOU WERE BORN TO BE.
> CAN'T YOU SEE
> THAT YOU'RE THE ONE AND ONLY YOU?

ALL.
> BE WHO YOU ARE...

QUARK.
> TO THINE OWN SELF BE TRUE!

> *(***QUARK** *riffs elaborately on the big note.)*

SPROCKET. *(Spoken in rhythm.)*
> IMPRESSIVE!

QUARK. *(Spoken in rhythm.)*
> THANKS!

> *(***QUARK** *bows with a flourish.)*

ALL.
> LET YOUR SPIRIT SOAR
> AS YOU FOLLOW YOUR OWN STAR.
> BE WHO YOU ARE.

> (**EARTHSULA** *appears, still trapped in the Black Hole.*)

EARTHSULA. Oh, sure! Just "be who you are" and that'll solve everything!

> I AM WHO I AM,
> AND THEN BAM! I GET SLAMMED
> IN THIS DARK, FORSAKEN VOID.

> I'LL BE BACK, AND YOU'LL SEE,
> YOU'LL BOW DOWN TO ME!
> YOUR DREAMS WILL BE DESTROYED!

> SO HAVE FUN.
> I PROMISE, ONE DAY
> I'LL RETURN, AND YOU'LL ALL SCRAM!
> YOU CAN'T BLAME ME –
> I AM WHO I AM!

> (**EARTHSULA** *exits.*)

QUARK. I can't believe she's gone.

SPROCKET. In the absence of your overseer, what do you intend to do?

QUARK. Gosh, I don't know! I could be a [funny object]! Or a [rare animal]! Or maybe [name of celebrity]!

SPROCKET. Quark...haven't you been listening?

> BE WHO YOU ARE...

SPROCKET & QUARK.
> BE WHATEVER IT IS THAT YOU WERE BORN TO BE.
> CAN'T YOU SEE
> THAT YOU'RE THE ONE AND ONLY YOU?

ALL (EXCEPT EARTHSULA).
>BE WHO YOU ARE...
>IN EV'RYTHING YOU DO!
>LET YOUR SPIRIT SOAR
>AS YOU FOLLOW YOUR OWN STAR...
>BE WHO YOU ARE!

>*(Optional: The actress playing* **EARTHSULA** *joins in as herself.)*

ALL.
>BE WHO YOU ARE...
>BE WHATEVER IT IS THAT YOU WERE BORN TO BE.
>CAN'T YOU SEE
>THAT YOU'RE THE ONE AND ONLY YOU?
>
>BE WHO YOU ARE...
>IN EV'RYTHING YOU DO!

GROUP 1.
>LET YOUR SPIRIT SOAR...

GROUP 2.
>GET WHAT YOU'RE HOPING FOR...

GROUP 3
>YOU'LL DO THAT AND MORE,

ALL.
>IF YOU FOLLOW YOUR OWN STAR.
>BE WHO YOU ARE!

The End

[MUSIC NO. 18 – BOWS (BE WHO YOU ARE)]